Chill

In memory of Brian Anson, friend, artist and storyteller.

Little Hare Books
an imprint of
Hardie Grant Egmont
Ground Floor, Building 1, 658 Church St
Richmond, Victoria 3121, Australia

www.littleharebooks.com

Cataloguing-in-Publication details are available from the
National Library of Australia

ISBN 978 1 921714 47 4 (pbk.)

Designed by Vida & Luke Kelly
Produced by Pica Digital, Singapore
Printed through Phoenix Offset
Printed in Shen Zhen, Guangdong Province, China, January 2012

5 4 3 2 1

Chill

Words and illustrations
by Carol Thompson

LITTLE HARE

www.littleharebooks.com

Dolly likes to play on her own.

Dum-di-dum-di-dum!

Especially the mirror game.

But some games are not much fun all alone.

Then ...

along comes Jack Rabbit,

Dolly's best friend in all the world.

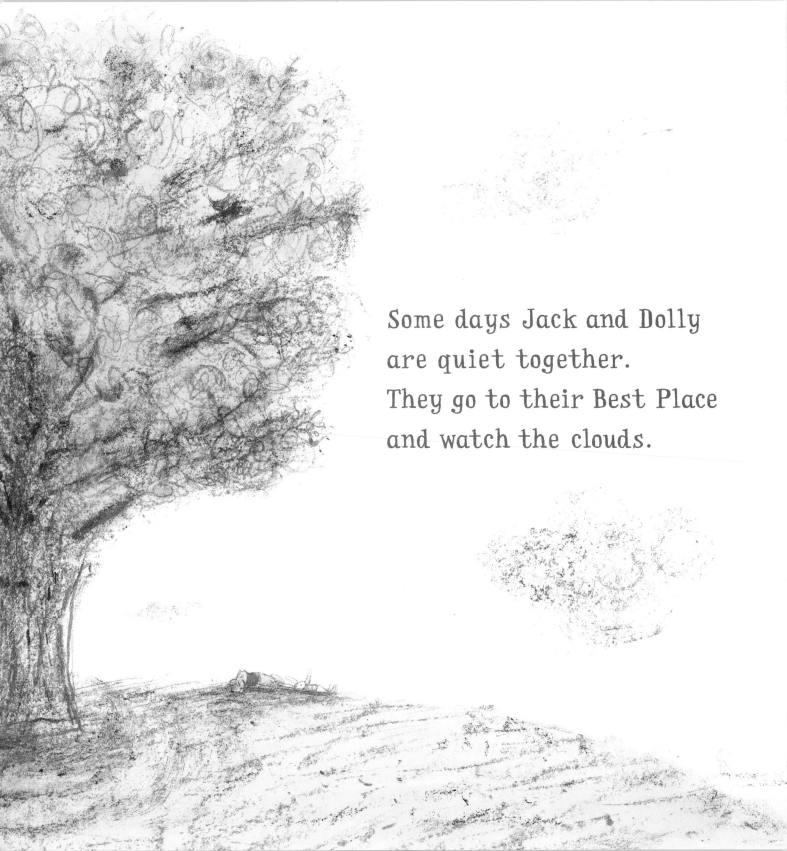

Some days Jack and Dolly
are quiet together.
They go to their Best Place
and watch the clouds.

Or listen to their favourite music.

Some days they race around so fast

and play so hard,

all they can do is . . .

LAUGH!

Jacky Knotty Noodle!

Dolly Wolly Doodle!

One day, when Dolly went to visit
Jack, he was wearing a beret.

Jack painted a big circle.
And then some smaller circles.
Dolly painted some long wobbly lines.

Dolly looked at Jack's picture.

Jack looked at Dolly's picture.

He's not my friend.

Jack's wrong.

I'm SAD ...

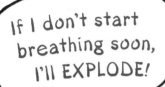

Dolly takes a deep breath.
All the way in and all the way out.

Dolly takes a
lovely warm bath.
She closes her
eyes and thinks
of something she
likes a lot.

Jack counts slowly up to ten,
and back down again.
And up again!

He closes his
eyes and thinks
of something he
likes a lot.

The next day ...

Dolly goes to her Best Place.

Jack goes to his Best Place.